D0459557

For Gabriela, who helps me see wonderful things
—S. M.

For my friends—
good helpers one and all.
—M. P.

Author's note: In Puerto Rican neighborhoods in the United States, a bodega is a grocery store, and one buys *piraqua*s (snow cones) and *coquito*s (coconut ices) from street vendors.

Atheneum Books for Young Readers • An imprint of Simon & Schuster Children's Publishing Division • 1230 Avenue of the Americas New York, New York 10020 • Text copyright © 2007 by Sonia Manzano • Illustrations copyright © 2007 by Matt Phelan • All rights reserved, including the right of reproduction in whole or in part in any form. • Book design by Sonia Chaghatzbanian and Debra Sfetsios • The text for this book is set in Stempel Schneidler. • The illustrations for this book are rendered in watercolor and pen and ink. • Manufactured in China • First Edition • 10 9 8 7 6 5 4 3 2 1 • Library of Congress Cataloging-in-Publication Data • Manzano, Sonia. • A box full of kittens / Sonia Manzano; illustrated by Matt Phelan.—1st ed. • p. cm. • Summary: When her aunt Juanita needs someone to run errands before the birth of her baby, Ruthie is excited to be able to help, but she is distracted by a surprise in the store and almost misses the big event. • ISBN-13: 978-0-689-83089-1 • ISBN-10: 0-689-83089-0 • [1. Helpfulness—Fiction. 2. Babies—Fiction. 3. Hispanic Americans—Fiction.] I. Phelan, Matt, ill. II. Title. • PZ7.M3213Bo 2007 • [E]—dc22 2006008607

a Box Full of Kittens

story by
Sonia Manzano

illustrations by **Matt Phelan**

ATHENEUM BOOKS FOR YOUNG READERS   NEW YORK   LONDON   TORONTO   SYDNEY

You never know when
something wonderful will happen.
I should know.

I'm Ruthie, and something wonderful
once happened to me.

It was a regular old day.

My papi had just fixed the
antenna on the television set,
so I could finish watching my
favorite show, *Superman*.

I love Superman.
I wish I could be Superman.
If I were Superman, I could save kittens
that got stuck on rooftops in a single bound.

I could—

"Ruthie." It was my mami interrupting my thoughts. "I've got a job for you. Your aunt Juanita is going to have her baby very soon, and she'd like some company. Why don't you go spend the day with her in case she needs anything."

"But I have to see what happens to Superman," I said.

"Don't worry," said my brother, Willy.
"He'll be okay. He has to be back
for next week's show. Heh, heh."

Willy thought he was a comedian.

"Why can't Willy stay with her?" I asked.

Then it hit me.

If I were the one to get help for Aunt Juanita,
I would be a hero, just like Superman.
"Never mind!" I hollered before Willy had a chance to answer.
"I'll stay with Aunt Juanita. Mami asked me first."

I flew out the door, down the steps (two at a time),
past Don Felix's bodega, past the man who sold *coquito* ices,
past the *piraquero* who sold snow cones,
into Aunt Juanita's building, up the steps (three at a time),
and finally leaped into Aunt Juanita's kitchen.

"Is it time for the baby to come?
Should I get help?" I asked my aunt.

"Not yet," she said, struggling to kiss me over her big belly.
She looked as if she had swallowed a beach ball.
"But could you go get me a cherry *piraqua*
with extra syrup? I really feel like having one."
She handed me some money from her purse.

I grabbed the money, flew out the door, down the steps (four at a time),
out onto the street, and ran to the *piraquero*.

"I need a cherry *piraqua* with extra syrup—quick!"

I gave him the money, grabbed the *piraqua*, ran back into Aunt Juanita's building,
flew up the steps (five at a time), and leaped into Aunt Juanita's kitchen.

"Well?" I asked, handing her the cone. "Is the baby coming? Do you feel it's time? Should I get help?"

"No," she said, between slurps of *piraqua*. "I don't feel the baby coming, but I do feel that after I eat this *piraqua*, I'm going to want a *coquito*. Could you take some money from the coffee can on the shelf and get me one? Extra large?"

I got the money, flew out the door, down the steps (six at a time),
out onto the street, past the *piraquero*, and up to the *coquito* vendor.

"Can I have an extra-large *coquito*—quick!"

I gave him the money, grabbed the *coquito*, ran back into my aunt's building,
flew up the steps (seven at a time), and landed in Aunt Juanita's kitchen
in a single bound.

"How about now?" I panted, completely out of breath.
"Do you think the baby is coming? Do you feel it's time?
Should I get help?"

"No," she said, biting
into the *coquito*,
"I don't feel the baby coming,
but I'm beginning to feel hungry for real food.

"Could you go to the bodega
and get me a piece of *queso blanco*
and *pasta de guayaba* to go with it?"
(That means "white cheese" and "guava paste"
in Spanish, in case you didn't know).
"Tell Don Felix I'll pay him later."

I got to Don Felix's store faster than the speed of light.

"Could I have a—"

But before I could finish he said,
"Ruthie, you'll never guess."

"Huh? What? Guess? I can't . . .
I'm in a hurry," I said.
"Could I have a—"

"You'll never believe what I have right here,"
he said, disappearing behind the counter.

"What? But there's a baby—," I began.

"Not just one. But three!" he said.

"Huh?"

He stood up, holding a big box.
"Take a look, take a look—you'll love it."

"I can't. I need a piece of—"

Don Felix opened the lid. "Look!"

I looked.

Inside the box were kittens.
Three little kittens.
I love kittens.
I love,
love,
love,
love,
love kittens.
And here were three tiny,
mewling kittens!

"These were almost just born," said Don Felix. "I've been waiting
for you to come by. I knew you'd want to see them."

"They're beautiful," I said. I couldn't believe my eyes.

"I knew you'd love them," he said. "Why don't you take them outside
for some fresh air?"

I hugged the box and went out
to the sidewalk. The kittens made the tiniest
sound I almost couldn't hear unless
I got really close.

I put the box on the sidewalk
and looked into it.

There was a peppy kitten, a mysterious kitten, and a
sleepy kitten. I couldn't decide which one to pick up first.
I went to pick up the peppy kitten, but the mysterious kitten
gave me such a look, I started to pick her up instead.
But then I didn't want the sleepy one to feel left out,
so I decided to pick them all up at the same time.

That made one climb up onto the top of my head,
one crawl up onto my shoulder, and one curl up,
right inside the crook of my elbow!
Then I heard my aunt Juanita yelling
something to me from her third-floor window.

"Yes, I know!" I whispered back loudly
(I didn't want to disturb the kittens).
"These are the cutest kittens in the world."

Then my aunt yelled something else.

"Okay!" I said, waving to her.
Boy, she must really be hungry, I thought.
"Be right there!"

Of course all that yelling upset the kittens. It made the sleepy one snuggle into my neck, the peppy one jump back into the box, and the mysterious one try to run away!

It was a good thing Officer Vic was coming up the sidewalk, because he was able to catch her for me.

"Thank you, Officer Vic! You're just in time to see these beautiful kittens!"

"Very nice," he said, handing the mysterious kitten back to me. But just as I was about to ask him which kitten he liked best, he started talking into his walkie-talkie and running into Aunt Juanita's building. Suddenly there was a loud noise, and all the kittens tried to climb onto my head.

"Don't worry, kittens,"
I whispered. "It's just a siren.
You'll hear a lot of those in this city.
There's nothing to be afraid of."
I tried to calm them down by petting them
all at the same time. Which is impossible
(in case you didn't know), because
they kept squirming around.

Then I saw my father coming down the street.
He was walking awfully fast. "Hey, Papi," I whispered importantly.
"Look at these kittens!"

"*ESPERATE!*" he said.

Wait? I thought. *Wait for what?*
I held the mysterious-looking kitten
up into the air to show Papi, but he
ran toward Aunt Juanita's building.

That's when I noticed
my aunt being helped into
an ambulance by Officer Vic.
The three kittens stared at me,
and I stared at the ambulance.

"Well," said my papi as he walked back toward me. "It's a good thing Officer Vic was around to help your aunt."

"Help my aunt . . . ?" I said.

"She's about to have her baby!" he answered.

"Now?" I asked him.

"Well, very soon," he said.

I stared at the ambulance as it pulled away from the curb.

"Hey, what have you got there?" he asked.

"Nothing," I said. "Just some old kittens. They're Don Felix's."

"Well, give them back, and let's go tell your mother that by tonight, there'll be a new member of the family."

I dragged myself up the stairs. One step at a time.

A few days later I was watching television (NOT *Superman*) when my mami said it was time to visit Aunt Juanita and her new baby, named Grace.

"Great," said my brother. "Hey, Ruthie, what's the difference between a baby and a leaky faucet?" Before I could answer, he said, "You can turn off a faucet! Get it? Ha, ha, ha!"

And before I had a chance *not* to laugh, my mother asked, "Why the long face, Ruthie? Honestly . . . Let's go."

We got to Aunt Juanita's apartment, along with the rest of the neighborhood.

The party started immediately. My father searched for a good Spanish station on the radio. My mother made the coffee and served the cake.

Officer Vic smiled at everything everybody said, even though I could tell he didn't understand much Spanish. Don Felix brought a whole salami. I hadn't brought anything. Besides, everyone was making such a fuss that I couldn't even get near baby Grace. I was just about to give up and go downstairs when I heard my aunt Juanita say, "I swear it was that *coquito* Ruthie brought me that made this baby finally come!"

"I knew it was something you ate," said my aunt's husband, Frank.

"Some things never change," said my great-uncle. "Why, I remember when my wife just *had* to chew on a piece of sugarcane right before she had our first son."

"I remember your great-aunt, Isabela, begging for coconut milk right before she gave birth," added my other great-uncle. "And if you don't think it's hard climbing a palm tree in the middle of the night, think again."

Everybody laughed but me.

"Well, it was a good thing Ruthie was around," Aunt Juanita declared. "She really saved the day. Ruthie, since you were so helpful with your superfast deliveries, you should be the first to hold the baby."

Everybody said, "Yes, of course," and stepped aside to let me through.

My aunt put the baby in my arms and showed me how to hold her, so her head wouldn't fall back. Grace's eyes were shut. But her hands fluttered a little as she got comfortable. She had the prettiest, newest fingers I had ever seen.

"Hello, Grace," I said.

She opened her eyes. Everyone gasped and stood on their tiptoes to get a better look. Then everyone sighed and settled down as she closed them again.

Then Grace made the tiniest sound that I almost couldn't hear unless I got really close. Which I did, because I knew she only wanted me to hear it.

And I finally felt super.

3 1901 05300 8472